PUFFIN BOOKS

GRIZZWOLD

After the man came to chop down trees in the forest, Grizzwold had to set out to find a new home. He tried the mountains, the prairies and the desert before he found the perfect spot.

New readers love to read proper stories, and they will certainly delight in the uproarious adventures of Grizzwold.

Also published by Puffin in the I C A N R E A D series is Syd Hoff's *Danny and the Dinosaur*, the story of a small boy who finds a dinosaur to take on a trip round the city.

The I CAN READ books

Grizzwold

Story and pictures by
Syd Hoff

PUFFIN BOOKS

Puffin Books, Penguin Books Ltd, Harmondsworth, Middlesex, England
Viking Penguin Inc., 40 West 23rd Street, New York, New York 10010, U.S.A.
Penguin Books Australia Ltd, Ringwood, Victoria, Australia
Penguin Books Canada Ltd, 2801 John Street, Markham, Ontario, Canada L3R 1B4
Penguin Books (N.Z.) Ltd, 182-190 Wairau Road, Auckland 10, New Zealand

First published in Great Britain by World's Work Ltd 1964
Published in Puffin Books 1983
Reprinted 1985

Copyright © Syd Hoff, 1963
All rights reserved

Printed and bound in Great Britain by
William Clowes Limited, Beccles and London

In the far North

lived a bear named Grizzwold.

Grizzwold was so big

three rabbits could sit in his footprint.

When he went fishing,

the river only came to his knees.

Other bears had no trouble

going into caves to sleep.

Grizzwold always got stuck.

He had to sleep out in the open.

But he didn't mind.

He had a nice coat of fur

to keep him warm.

No other animal dared wake him.

One morning there was a loud noise
in the forest.

All the other bears ran away.

Grizzwold went to see what it was.

He saw men chopping down trees.

"Timber!" they shouted.

"What's the big idea?" asked Grizzwold.

"What are you doing to my forest?"

"We are sorry," said the men.

"We have to send these logs

down the river to the mill.

They will be made into paper."

15

"I can't live in a forest
with no trees," said Grizzwold.

He went to look

for a new place to live.

"Do you know

where there is a nice forest?"

he asked.

"You won't find one up here,"
said a mountain goat.

19

"Do you know

where there is a nice forest?"

he asked.

"You won't find one here,"

said a prairie wolf.

"Do you know

where there is a nice forest?"

he asked.

"Well, you are lost!"

said a desert lizard.

23

Grizzwold looked until he saw houses.

"What can I do here?" he asked.

"You can be a bearskin rug,"
said some people.

They let him into their house.

Grizzwold lay down on the floor.

The people stepped all over him.

"Ow! I don't like this," said Grizzwold.

29

He left the house.

Grizzwold saw a lamp-post.

"I'll climb that tree," he said.

31

"I was here first," said a cat.

He chased Grizzwold away.

Grizzwold saw a dog.

"Can't you read?" asked the dog.

He chased Grizzwold away.

Grizzwold saw people going to a dance.

The people wore masks.

36

Grizzwold went to the dance too.

"You look just like a real bear,"
said the people.

"Thank you," said Grizzwold.

The people started to dance.

Grizzwold started to dance too.

"It is time to take off our masks,"
said somebody.

All the people took off their masks.

"Take off yours too,"

they said to Grizzwold.

"I can't," he said.

"This is my real face."

"You don't belong here,"

said the people.

"You belong in the zoo."

Grizzwold went to the zoo.

45

The bears were begging for peanuts.

Grizzwold begged too.

"Please don't stay," said the bears.

"We need all the peanuts we get.

Try the circus."

Grizzwold went to the circus.

They put skates on him.

He went FLOP!

They put him on a bicycle.

He went CRASH!

They tried to make him

stand on his head.

He couldn't do that either!

"I suppose it takes practice,"

said Grizzwold.

"It certainly does," said the trained bears.

Grizzwold tried to rest.

"You can't park here,"

said a traffic warden.

"I'll find a place to park,"

said Grizzwold.

He ran until he came to a nice forest.

"I'm very glad to be here," he said.

"We are very glad you are here too,"

said some hunters.

They took aim.

"Don't shoot!" said a game warden.

"This is a game reserve.

No guns allowed."

The hunters left.

"Thank you," said Grizzwold.

"You will be safe here,"

said the warden.

"People cannot shoot animals here.

They can only take pictures."'"

All the people

wanted to take Grizzwold's picture.

He was the biggest bear

they had ever seen.

They gave him all

the peanuts he could eat.

"This is the life for me,"

said Grizzwold.

He was very happy.